E-BOY

ANH DO

E-BOY

Illustrations by Chris Wahl

ALLEN&UNWIN
SYDNEY•MELBOURNE•AUCKLAND•LONDON

First published by Allen & Unwin in 2020

Allen & Unwin
83 Alexander Street
Crows Nest NSW 2065
Australia
Phone: (61 2) 8425 0100
Email: info@allenandunwin.com
Web: www.allenandunwin.com

 A catalogue record for this
book is available from the
National Library of Australia

ISBN 978 1 76087 752 1

For teaching resources, explore www.allenandunwin.com/resources/
for-teachers

Cover design by Jo Hunt and Chris Wahl
Text design by Jo Hunt
Set in 13/22 pt Legacy Serif by Midland Typesetters

Printed and bound in Australia by McPherson's Printing Group

10 9 8 7 6 5 4 3 2 1

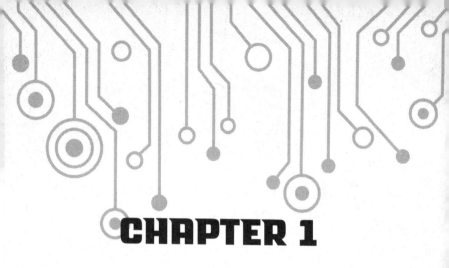

CHAPTER 1

I hate me! Ethan thought to himself.

I hate this stupid body, I hate this hospital, I hate everything!!!

Ethan's angry thoughts swirled around his head as he lay on the operating table in nothing but his underwear.

He considered running out of the room, but he knew he didn't look great in those tight white undies. That was enough to keep him lying there, awaiting his fourteenth operation in eighteen months.

The storm raging outside didn't help his mood. Lightning flashed through the windows, glinting off the medical machines around him.

Ethan tried to calm himself . . . *You should be used to hospitals by now*, he thought. *You've spent enough time in them.*

Throughout his childhood he had been plagued with health problems – heart, bone and muscle issues – but, after years of treatments, he thought he'd finally beaten them all.

In his mid-teens Ethan had, for the first time in his life, found himself relatively strong, and able to be . . . normal. He'd made friends, played sport, and to everyone's surprise, including his own, he got a girlfriend.

He'd also been able to concentrate on his true calling, computer coding, and his brilliant marks had allowed him to graduate school early and take up a scholarship to a top computing course at Titan University.

Then the terrible headaches began, followed by the devastating diagnosis of an inoperable brain tumour.

'This looks worse than anyone predicted,' a nurse muttered. Ethan worried she was talking about him, then realised she meant the storm.

'How you holding up there, Ethan?'

Doctor Penny Cook appeared beside him. Her presence was calming, transforming his fear into mere awkwardness.

He felt embarrassed as he lay there, near-naked. He was thin and gangly, and half his hair was shaved off. He didn't exactly feel handsome.

He knew it was silly to get a crush on an older woman – especially his doctor – but he couldn't help it.

Doctor Cook had chestnut hair and deep brown eyes, and her smooth skin was pale from years spent under fluorescent lights in laboratories.

I might die within the hour, he thought. *I can have a crush on whoever I like.*

When Ethan's tumour had been diagnosed, his parents consulted the best doctors in the world. They all said it was impossible to cure him. Then Penny had appeared, like an angel in a shining white lab coat.

She was a prodigy, a leading global expert in neuroscience and artificial intelligence at just twenty-six years of age. She had heard about Ethan's condition and approached his parents to ask if he was willing to try a highly experimental procedure involving a medical android she'd created.

Given his only other option was to die, Ethan had agreed. Now he found himself in a state-of-the-art government medical facility. He'd had to sign dozens of secrecy agreements and go through all kinds of security checks to get inside.

So had his parents, who were waiting outside the operating room.

'Ethan?' Penny said. 'You lost in thought?'

'Kinda.'

'It's perfectly natural to be anxious,' said Penny, putting a hand on his arm, 'but we'll get you through this.'

Ethan smiled weakly. She couldn't possibly be as certain as she sounded. Not when this was the first time this procedure had ever been attempted.

'Now,' said Penny, 'I believe you've met Gemini.'

The medical android stepped into Ethan's view.

He looks so . . . perfect, thought Ethan.

With short blond hair, angular features and lithe frame, Gemini was almost indistinguishable from a man in his mid-twenties. What gave him away were his chrome eyes, and the power

cable reaching from his back into a control panel.

Gemini was a groundbreaking creation, unknown to the public, and one of the reasons Ethan had to sign all those stay-quiet forms. Penny hoped Gemini would revolutionise the medical industry.

'Hello, Ethan.' Gemini's mouth curved upwards in what was supposed to be a reassuring smile, but actually looked a bit creepy. 'Good to see you again. Are you ready to begin?'

'Do you think it will work?' asked Ethan.

'I have a one hundred per cent surgical success rate,' Gemini said. 'However, this procedure is untested. I calculate a probability of—'

'That's enough, Gemini,' Penny interrupted. She shot Ethan an apologetic look. 'His bedside manner needs a little tweaking.'

'Just give me the anaesthetic already,' Ethan said bluntly, and immediately regretted his tone.

'All right, Ethan.' Penny reached for the IV attached to his arm and twisted the valve.

As his eyes grew heavier, Ethan wondered if he would ever open them again.

'Just give me the anaesthetic already,' weren't exactly great last words. He needed to say something better before his tongue went numb.

'Don't screw this up, guys,' he mumbled to Penny and Gemini. *Not a whole lot better!*

The thunder outside sounded like the sky ripping itself apart.

CHAPTER 2

'Subject is unconscious,' said Gemini. 'Permission to commence procedure?'

As Penny sat behind a semicircle of monitors, she wondered if the assurances she'd given Ethan were for him or her. She reminded herself that Ethan had no chance at all without her and Gemini.

Via the monitors, Penny watched as Gemini raised his right hand and tiny panels opened

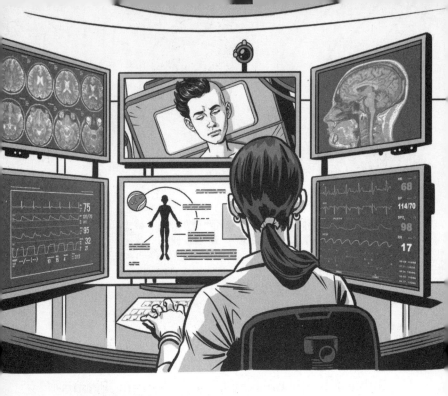

on the tips of his fingers, each revealing a laser scalpel. With five scalpels working together, Gemini could make multiple incisions simultaneously and with inhuman precision.

'Proceed,' she said.

Gemini positioned his fingers over Ethan's scalp, and bright blue, incredibly thin lasers sprang out. Gemini started to cut.

Penny tried not to think about Ethan's
parents, waiting outside, as Gemini worked
quickly and methodically. More surgical equipment emerged from his fingers, including
forceps, pincers and a tiny mirror.

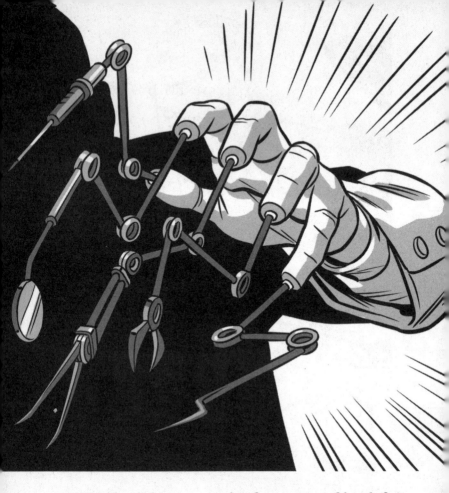

Panels slid open on the fingertips of his left hand now, and tiny silver rods extended. At the end of these rods were nano-tools, allowing Gemini to work at a microscopic level no human surgeon could ever achieve.

The aim was to remove Ethan's advanced tumour then reconnect severed synapses, some-thing previously untried in medical science.

'Status update?' said Penny.

'Proceeding to excise the tumour.'

Gemini worked quickly. As instruments popped in and out of him, he could cut, stem bleeding and perform dozens of tiny operations simultaneously.

As Penny watched him, her confidence returned. Gemini was working around the tumour easily. However, the trickiest part was yet to come.

A peal of thunder startled Penny as Gemini dropped the tumour into a jar.

'Tumour excised,' he said. 'Permission to commence reconnecting synaptic pathways?'

Gemini was effectively about to rewire Ethan's brain.

'Proceed,' Penny said, trying to keep her voice steady.

Gemini began reconnecting the millions of neural pathways in Ethan's brain.

Penny scanned Ethan's brain on the monitor. In the sections that Gemini had repaired, Ethan's brain was firing as normal.

Two hours later, Ethan's heart was beating normally and the damage to his brain was almost reversed.

'One per cent connections remaining,' said Gemini.

The windows lit up as lightning cracked.

Then came a great zapping noise from above.

The nurses glanced at each other. 'What was that?' Penny asked them urgently.

'I think the building's been struck!' said one of the nurses.

Penny's monitors flickered and she pulled back her fingers in alarm as her keyboard sparked.

The lights in the ceiling exploded, raining down shards of glass. Bands of pure energy rippled along Gemini's cord from the control panel.

'No!' shouted Penny.

Electricity surged into Gemini. His back arched as white-hot bands travelled down his arms and passed directly into Ethan! Ethan convulsed, his muscles contracting as the power coursed through him.

For a moment, everything fell silent, save the rain battering the windows.

Then the machinery whirred back to life, illuminating the room in a blinking, haphazard way. Gemini was slumped over the table, Ethan still beneath him.

Penny's heart sank – surely no one could survive an electrical shock directly to the brain.

Suddenly Gemini lurched back into action. He straightened, then hastily started stitching up Ethan's scalp.

'Is he alive?' said Penny.

'Unknown,' said Gemini.

Penny ran to Ethan's side and put two fingers on his wrist.

There was a pulse!

CHAPTER 3

'Ethan?'

The first thing Ethan was aware of was Penny's face above his. His eyes shot open so fast he made her startle.

'I'm alive?'

'Seems so,' Penny said, smiling with relief.

Ethan was lying in a bed that was a lot more comfortable than the one in the operating theatre. There was a slight throbbing in his head.

'How do you feel?' asked Penny.

Ethan sat up. He felt alert, awake . . . good! He could hardly believe it.

'Did you remove the tumour?' he asked.

'Yes . . . but there was a complication.' Penny gently eased him back down.

'Complication? That's never good,' Ethan said.

'It was a freak occurrence. The top of the building was hit by lightning, which caused a power surge. Gemini was electrocuted while he was operating. And so were you.'

'Whoa,' Ethan said. 'My brain was fried?'

'Actually . . . no,' said Penny. 'I've been running scans all night and . . . well, it seems that you suffered no damage from the electrocution. You're cured!'

'Best complication ever!' Ethan said. 'Have you told my parents? They must be worried sick.'

'I've told them you're alive. Now that I can see you're . . . still you . . . I'll let them in.'

As Penny made a call, Ethan gazed at the heart monitor. The line spiked in sync with his heartbeat, beeping each time. Ethan found the beep annoying, so he reached out, hoping to find the volume button.

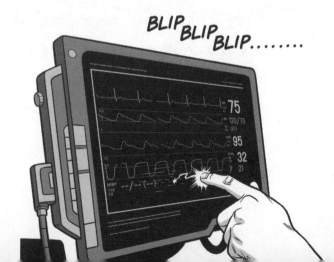

But as soon his hand touched the machine his eyes glazed over and he drifted into what felt like a waking dream. The heart monitor was full of electrical pathways governed by a CPU . . . all he had to do was perform a quick tweak to its algorithms . . .

'Ethan?!' Penny rushed back to the bedside, alarmed.

'What is it?' he asked.

'The monitor stopped beeping . . . but you're okay. Hmm. Maybe the storm damaged the equipment.'

Ethan looked at the heart monitor in confusion. The line still spiked, but the machine wasn't beeping anymore. He couldn't have done that, could he? Maybe imagining things was a side effect of the operation?

The door burst open and his mum and dad rushed in. Tracy and Paul Forrester wore expressions of relief.

'Oh, my boy!' His mum threw her arms around him. 'I was so worried.'

'Careful, Tracy,' said his father, holding back. 'The kid's just had major brain surgery.'

Ethan could see that his dad wanted to hug him too, so he smiled. 'It's fine, Dad. I actually feel pretty great.'

He managed to pull an arm free of his mother and held it out to his father, who didn't need any more encouragement. Carefully, Paul wrapped his arms around his wife and son.

Soon everyone was crying. Ethan had so many tears on his face, he wasn't sure which were his and which were his parents'.

'It's okay, guys,' he told them. 'I'm okay.'

Penny waved goodbye as Paul and Tracy got into the elevator with Ethan. She would rather keep him in for observation, but all his vitals were excellent. So Penny had settled for a promise that Ethan would call her daily, and come back for a check-up soon.

As the doors closed, Ethan caught her gaze through the tangle of parental affection.

'Thank you,' he mouthed.

Penny smiled warmly, then walked back to her lab. She would have to run diagnostics on all her devices, including Gemini, before they could be used again.

When Penny arrived, she was irritated to find a man in a suit waiting for her. A man she didn't like.

'Agent Ferris,' she said.

Agent Ferris was middle-aged, with oversized square glasses and closely cropped black hair. His suit bore no government insignia, but she knew he was a People's Service Agent assigned to watch over her.

'Doctor Cook, I hear the Gemini model was successful again . . . even after having a thousand volts shot through him!'

Penny hoped if she kept her answers brief this would be over soon. 'He was.'

Ferris moved over to Gemini, who was powered down. 'Very impressive. And no damage to our favourite android?'

'I don't think so,' said Penny. 'I want to run some tests.'

'My superiors are very eager to see the robot tested in the field,' said Ferris. 'The situation in Sharo is worsening every day, and our troops would benefit greatly from such a highly skilled surgeon. In your last update you mentioned you'd been working on a new battery to make him more mobile. How's that coming along?'

'A day or two more, and I'll have it installed.'

Agent Ferris flashed a row of straight white teeth that made him look like a bespectacled shark. 'Excellent,' he said. 'Make it your top priority. I want to ship Gemini out by Tuesday.'

'Tuesday?' said Penny. 'But there's still much to be tested. His software, his core personality . . .'

'I can tell you that wounded soldiers won't care a jot about his personality,' said Ferris. 'So long as he gets them back on their feet.'

'That's not what I meant—' said Penny.

'I shouldn't have to remind you that the government has paid for everything here. Now they want results. Tuesday, Doctor Cook.'

Ferris strode out the door without waiting for her reply.

Penny chewed her lip. Was Gemini ready for the outside world? She wasn't sure... but it didn't seem like she had any say in it.

CHAPTER 4

Ethan could not believe his speedy recovery. Just a day after surgery, he was back in one of his favourite places: the computer lab at Titan University. Sitting beside him were his old schoolfriends, Stevie J and Rose. They were boyfriend and girlfriend – Stevie was short and quiet with long brown hair, and Rose was tall and loud, with dyed hair.

'Yo,' said Rose, tapping on her keyboard. 'He just turned off Gardeners Road.'

'Man,' said Stevie J with a grin, 'that's going to put him in the middle of nowhere.'

They were practising their hacking skills. They never did anything really dangerous or scammed anyone. For Ethan, the sheer thrill of cracking in was the reward, but a little mischief didn't go astray.

To celebrate Ethan's return, the trio had decided to mess around with a bully they went to school with. Brad Larson had given them a really hard time for being geeks. Now he had a job driving a van for Hyperspeed Couriers.

They had hacked into the Hyperspeed network and sent Brad to a strange address to pick up a package that didn't exist.

Ethan watched the blip on a GPS map: Brad driving through a barren industrial zone.

'I think I can access some security cams in there,' he said.

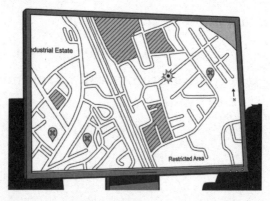

Stevie J and Rose looked worried. The city's camera network was tightly controlled by the government.

'You sure that's a good idea?' said Rose.

Ethan's fingers danced across the keyboard. He didn't know why, but since the surgery, hacking had become a whole lot easier. It was like the code spoke to him.

'Yeah, it's fine,' he said, as he typed commands that would hide his IP address. 'Besides, we're just having a look. Check it out!'

He clicked his fingers, and the security footage flicked up on all three monitors.

SNAP!

'Whoa!' Stevie J exclaimed.

'How did you do that?' asked Rose. 'You need our permission to put something on our screens.'

Ethan frowned. 'Must have accessed some command for it. Anyway, look, there he is!'

The camera showed a Hyperspeed Couriers van pulling up at a plumbing supplies warehouse. Brad looked confused as he got out of the van and walked towards the entrance.

Brad moved inside the warehouse and out of camera range.

'Oh man, wish we could see his face,' Stevie J said.

'We can.' Ethan concentrated on the screen as his fingers flew over the keys. A moment later, the view from a camera inside the warehouse foyer flickered onto all of their screens. Ethan even managed to access audio.

'You're on fire today!' Rose said.

The three of them watched Brad walk up to the reception desk and ring the bell.

A sweaty man appeared from the back of the warehouse. 'What do you want?'

'I'm from Hyperspeed Couriers,' said Brad. 'I'm here to pick up . . .' He referred to his palm tablet. '. . . um, three crates of bananas. It says they must be ripe.'

The hairy man scoffed. 'Does this look like a banana factory to you?'

Stevie J giggled.

'Well, no, but it says here . . .'

'Kid, I don't care what it says, we're working round the clock to fill a big order. We don't have time for this nonsense.'

'Look,' Brad said, showing the man the tablet. 'It says right here – three crates of bananas, to be picked up from this address, care of Reginald Doonside.'

'Reginald Doonside? I think someone's playing a joke on you, son.'

The man disappeared back into the warehouse and Brad stalked out the door.

Ethan switched the view back to street level as Brad returned to his van.

'Poor Brad,' laughed Rose.

'Wonder if he'll get in trouble from his boss?' Stevie J said.

'Let's find out,' said Ethan. Code streamed towards him, as if he was flying through a vortex of bits and bytes. He whizzed from the national network to Brad's provider to Brad's phone.

He then switched on the phone's internal microphone.

'How are you doing that?' asked Stevie.

Ethan blinked and glanced down at his

hands. They were resting on the keyboard, but he couldn't remember if he had actually been typing. Rose was staring at him.

'Um . . .'

'But I'm telling you,' snapped Brad, 'I have the order right here!'

From the other end of the call came an unsympathetic voice. 'Brad, there's nothing in the system about a warehouse on Gardeners Road, let alone three crates of bananas. Now get back to work!' Brad's boss hung up, and Brad cursed in frustration.

Ethan felt bad for him. The guy had been seriously unpleasant at school, but Ethan didn't want him to get fired. He squinted at his computer and shut everything down.

'Hey!' exclaimed Rose, as the vision disappeared off their screens.

'Sorry,' said Ethan. He realised that he still wasn't typing, so he bashed the keyboard for show.

He didn't know what was happening to him, but whatever it was, he wasn't ready to share it with his friends just yet. He needed to investigate alone.

'Gotta go!' Ethan scooped up his bag and left Stevie J and Rose staring at each other, gobsmacked.

CHAPTER 5

'Hi Mum and Dad,' Ethan sang out as he hurried towards his room. He was desperate to get to his computer, to explore this *feeling*, of being in tune with the machine.

'Perfect timing, Ethan. Dinner's ready,' Tracy called back.

'Now?!' Ethan was annoyed at being inter-rupted at this incredible moment. But he chased the feeling away.

'Coming,' he called.

Testing his powers would have to wait, at least until after dinner.

When he entered the kitchen, his parents both beamed at him. Having a carefree family meal wouldn't be such a big deal to many people, but to his parents it meant the world.

As they sat down to eat, his mum tuned her digital radio to a pop music station. An annoying repetitive song came on.

Oooh yeah, you turn me on! went the chorus.

I'll do the opposite of that, thought Ethan.

He concentrated on the radio until he made sense of its internal systems, then tuned it to a classical music station instead.

'Thing must be on the blink,' said Tracy, getting up to have a look at it.

'Mum?' said Ethan. 'Can we leave it on this station? I find Mozart kinda soothing.'

Tracy smiled and sank back into her chair. 'Of course, dear.'

Ethan felt a touch guilty about manipulating his mother, but it had been a *very* annoying pop song.

He noticed the household router sitting on the kitchen counter. It pulsed at him, almost like it was saying hello.

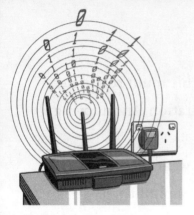

As Ethan stared at it, he saw a silver stream of data shooting through the walls of the house. He instinctively latched onto it and was suddenly *whooshed* along at incredible speed.

The stream split into more streams, which split into more streams, which became myriad complicated fractals . . . full of possibilities!

He floated above it for a moment, marvelling at the flashing web of data, a trillion threads crisscrossing the entire planet.

Wow, he thought, *surfing the net really is like surfing.*

He could sense everything in the house that contained a computer chip. His computer, his phone, a remote control car, even his alarm clock. It was amazing how many things were controlled by chips these days!

What was even more amazing was he could see their code too, like coloured strings interweaving in ways that he could instantly comprehend and change.

Whatever had happened to his brain during the operation had given him the ability to manipulate any computer.

Something drew his perception back to his body, like the power cord being sucked back into a vacuum cleaner. It was not a pleasant feeling. Suddenly, he was looking at his dad's face.

'Ethan? You haven't touched your meal,' Paul said, looking worried.

It was taking Ethan a moment to truly return to his body, as if threads of himself were still being reeled in. He felt . . . stretched.

'I think I was just . . . having a bad daydream. Sorry, Dad.'

'That's okay, mate,' Paul said, a little relieved.

Ethan didn't have an appetite, but he knew it would make his parents happy to see him eating heartily. Forcing a smile, he began to cut up a fritter.

As he ate, Ethan couldn't stop thinking about his newfound powers. From years of watching superhero movies and reading comic books, he knew that new heroes often spent ages wondering why this had happened to them, and often got all angsty about it.

Not going to make that mistake, Ethan thought. Instead, he felt a great curiosity and eagerness building inside him.

CHAPTER 6

The next day, Ethan and his mum went for a walk to the shops. Ethan was tired, but he enjoyed the sun on his face. They bought a bunch of groceries and waited at the lights for the green man. It seemed to take forever.

Ethan could easily reach into the city's traffic network and speed things up, but he knew a small tweak could result in consequences for motorists and pedestrians everywhere.

Just stand here with your mum, he told himself. *Like a normal human being.*

'Got plans tonight?' Tracy asked.

Ethan frowned. He knew what she was really asking. Ever since his high school girlfriend had broken up with him, he hadn't had an amazing dating life. Tracy always told him he was handsome, but what did mums know?

Doctor Penny's face floated into his mind. What was she doing tonight? *Probably not hanging out with boys ten years younger than her.*

The light turned green and they stepped onto the road. Ethan heard Tracy gasp, and turned to see a truck bearing down on them – the driver had sped up to run the red light!

Time seemed to slow down.

Ethan saw his mum's face fill with fear as she threw her hand across his chest – as if that would stop four tonnes of oncoming steel.

He saw the truck driver's eyes open wide and felt a surge of anger – the stupid man had put all their lives in danger just to save a few seconds. The driver slammed on the brakes and the tyres squealed as smoke shot out the sides, but he was never going to slow down in time.

Ethan plunged into the truck's electronic systems – radio, engine, air conditioning – and spread himself out in every direction, looking for anything that might help. He found an electronic petrol gauge and diverted power to it from everywhere else, overloading it instantly.

There was a *BOOM* and the side of the truck exploded. The whole rig blew sideways and tipped over. It *screeeeeched* along the ground, sparks flying.

'Oh my god, are you okay?' Tracy clutched at Ethan as the spinning wheels missed their heads by centimetres.

As his mum pawed at him, Ethan felt a bunch of stuff all at once. Relief, white-hot rage at the driver, and annoyance at his mum for grasping him.

'I'm fine, Mum,' he said, pushing her hand away.

Tracy was so full of adrenaline she hardly noticed his reaction.

People ran towards them, calling out to ask whether they were okay. A couple of guys helped the driver climb out of the overturned cabin.

The man's face was pale and his hands were shaking.

'Get away from the truck!' someone yelled. The truck was oozing smoke from its side and plumes of fire were shooting upwards.

Ethan quickly looked into its systems and rerouted all the dangerous elements away from each other.

'Quick!' Tracy pulled at him.

'Get off me!' Ethan shouted. He picked up the grocery bags and strode off.

His mum blinked in hurt and confusion, then followed.

Ethan cursed silently. Why was he behaving this way to his mother? This wasn't him.

'I'm sorry for yelling,' he said. 'I just got a fright.'

'You and me both,' she said, looking back at the smoking truck.

Back home, Ethan tried to process everything. He felt tightly wound, stressed, tired and irritable, as if he had pushed himself too hard. There was a cost, it seemed, for electronic telepathy.

He smiled at the thought – had he just named his power?

The smile was short-lived. He desperately needed to confide in someone, and there was only one person he could think of. The woman who had been there when his mind was zapped by lightning. A doctor with a special understanding of the human brain.

Ethan took out his phone and called her number.

'Hi there, this is Penny. I'm unavailable for a few days, so please leave a message.'

Unavailable? thought Ethan. *But you made me promise to call daily.*

He tried to delve into Penny's phone to track its GPS, but it was switched off.

'Where are you, Doctor Penny?' he muttered.

Ethan set up an automated notification to let him know when Penny turned her GPS back on.

In the meantime, he was on his own.

CHAPTER 7

Across the world, in the Sharo Desert, a supply truck rumbled along a sandy road. Ahead was a brick compound, its walls manned by guards with machine guns that glinted in the sunshine. As the truck drew near, the driver said a string of numbers into his radio. The iron compound gate slowly opened.

The truck juddered as it hit a bump in the road.

Suddenly a hand sprang from the sand and clamped onto the truck's undercarriage.

The owner of the hand burst from the sand and hauled himself underneath the truck.

The truck hurtled through the gates, which closed behind it with a clang.

Gemini boosted power to his hands and feet to keep himself steady as he clung to the underside of the truck. Meanwhile, the radio receiver inside his head crackled with the voice of his commander.

'Good work, Gemini,' said General Mawson. 'They failed to detect you. Now remember, your priority is the hostages. There are ten of our citizens in there. You have a duty of care to see them safely returned home.'

Gemini wondered about this inefficient use of the General's breath. He had already given

Gemini his orders. Didn't Mawson know that a robot never forgets?

'Gemini, you hear me?'

Affirmative. Gemini's reply appeared as text on Mawson's command centre screen.

The truck parked in the middle of the compound courtyard. The driver got out while soldiers opened the back, speaking in a foreign language. Luckily Gemini was programmed with every language known to humanity.

'I was expecting more warheads,' a man said.

'This was all they had,' said the driver.

Gemini heard something hit the ground nearby, and glanced over. A gob of spit lay on the earth centimetres from his head. He narrowed his chrome eyes.

DNA scan in progress.

A moment later his analysis concluded: *Subject identified as Reno Belic, currently wanted in 16 countries.*

'Mawson here again,' said the General, completely unnecessarily. Gemini could cross-check the voice records of anyone who had ever spoken to him. 'You now have a secondary objective, Gemini – terminate Reno Belic.'

Gemini felt the order sink into his programming. He was compelled to follow it, despite the fact that it was completely at odds with his primary function as a medical practitioner. There seemed to be contradictions in his code.

Am I doing what I'm supposed to be? he wondered. The thought seemed to curl around inside him before being . . . *absorbed* . . . into his program. He wondered about that too. Were his own thoughts meant to add to his code?

This thought went into his code in turn.

Am I thinking independent thoughts? Gemini felt confusion for the first time.

'I demanded three times this many warheads,' said Reno, as his boots moved around the truck. 'And we shall get them – presuming they want to see their countrymen again. It's time I paid our hostages a visit.'

Gemini opened his mouth and a tiny silver orb flew out and latched onto Reno's boot. It was a mobile probe designed by Penny to access vision of a patient's passageways, but it doubled as a tracker.

'Gemini,' said Mawson, 'you have a better chance of getting those hostages out safely if there are no hostiles left alive.'

Gemini pondered this input.

When he woke up twenty-four hours ago with no memory, he knew in his core – quite

literally, his computer core – that he was a healer. This seemed at odds with his current directives. Did innocent lives take priority over the lives of those with evil intentions? Like killing bacteria to stop an infection? Or was it always wrong to take a life?

These questions spawned more bits of code.

Gemini watched the legs of the men unloading the truck. There were five men.

He splayed his fingers and an aperture opened in his palm. A syringe full of fast-acting anaesthetic snaked out on a prehensile cord. Gemini calculated speed and distance, then sent the syringe to jab repeatedly at the legs around the truck. There was swearing, cursing, confusion – and then all five men dropped unconscious to the ground.

Gemini rolled out from under the truck and onto his feet.

'This seems like an appropriate compromise,' he told the unconscious men.

A quick sweep with his enhanced eyes revealed no other heat signatures nearby. He walked in the same direction as Reno, through a stone archway and into a dark tunnel.

He came to a metal door, which was slightly ajar, and heard Reno's voice on the other side.

'. . . pay for your country's crimes, but do not fret. If they deliver us what we ask for, a few of you might walk away alive.'

Gemini could hear the man pacing. He isolated three other sources of footsteps. So, it was Reno and three guards inside. He could also hear stifled breathing and moans – it sounded like the hostages were gagged.

'Maybe I should kill one of you to show them I am serious,' said Reno. Gemini heard a woman's muffled cry.

There was no more time. His orders and his programming combined to push away other thoughts. It was his duty to save lives.

He wrenched open the door.

Ten hostages were heaped in the middle of the floor. Standing around them were Reno and his brutes, machine guns slung casually over their shoulders. One of them stood facing away from Gemini.

Gemini lunged forward and clapped his hands over the man's temples, knocking him unconscious. The other soldiers reached for their guns.

Gemini charged with inhuman speed and leapt at two of them as they raised their muzzles. He spun in the air as his laser scalpels flashed out from his fingertips.

As he landed, the men dropped to the floor on either side of him.

Power reserves at 90%.

'Kill him!' Reno yelled to the last guard.

Gemini stepped forward and grabbed the muzzle of the gun being swung towards him. He jabbed its butt into the guard, who flew backwards, leaving Gemini holding the gun.

'Please, don't shoot,' said Reno, backing away, his hands raised.

Gemini crushed the muzzle of the gun in his grip and flung it away.

'Do you surrender?' he asked.

Reno nodded frantically, but the way his eyes darted about told Gemini there was a high probability he was lying. Sure enough, the man produced a pistol and fired.

Gemini quickly turned to the side, making himself a smaller target.

CRUSH!

The bullet caught his elbow, ripping through his synthetic skin, then pinging off his cybernetic frame.

Gemini dropped to the floor and sent out a sweeping kick that took Reno's feet out from under him. Gemini knew the force of the fall would not be enough to reduce Reno's threat level to zero, so he pushed Reno's head to the ground. It met the stone floor with an almighty crack.

Reno Belic was dead.

Secondary objective complete, he sent to Mawson.

'Woohoo! Great going, Gemini.'

The General's jubilation seemed at odds with the grave nature of the situation. Death was not something to be celebrated, surely?

Gemini drew himself up and inspected his elbow. It was only superficial damage, but he was curious to see what he looked like under his synthetic skin. He was surprised to discover his frame was bright pink.

He turned to the terrified hostages.

'Please remain calm,' he said. He began to move among them, cutting their bonds with his laser scalpels. Two of them were injured – a woman with a wound on her brow, and a young man with a broken arm. Gemini set to work, using nano-instruments and micro-stitches to stop the woman's bleeding, and a syringe of anaesthetic to ease the man's pain.

He accessed his bank of expressions to see if he could find one to calm everyone down. His mouth stretched wide while his chrome eyes flashed.

Several of the hostages flinched away. *Might need to practise that one,* Gemini thought to himself. He returned his face to a neutral expression as he examined the man's broken arm.

'This will hurt,' said Gemini, 'but it will aid your recovery. Are you ready?'

The man nodded nervously. *Crunch!* Gemini snapped his bone back into alignment.

The man howled in pain. 'Who ... who are you?'

'I am a Gemini model android, a state-of-the-art medical professional.'

'Oh. Well thanks, Gemini,' the man said, then passed out.

CHAPTER 8

'One hundred per cent complete success!' exclaimed General Mawson, slapping Gemini hard on the back.

SLAP!

Gemini calculated that the force of the back slap was greater than necessary to convey congratulations. He felt something stir deep within, but it was gone before he could process it.

'Happy to serve, General,' he said.

Gemini glanced around the control room. Officers stood at computer terminals, where screens flashed up information and satellite pictures. It all seemed somehow familiar, though he could not remember ever being here.

'Has my memory been wiped?' he asked.

Mawson glanced uncomfortably at a couple of tech officers. Gemini wondered if he needed to work on his subtlety.

'Ah,' Mawson said. 'Yes, we've had to reboot you a few times. Just ironing out the kinks in your program. We only do it because you're a vital asset to our operations, Gemini.'

Gemini watched the man's eyes. Flickering indicated the high probability of a lie.

Did all humans lie? And why would Mawson lie about this? Gemini was bound to carry out his orders. He could not act of his own free will. Unless Mawson suspected Gemini was more than just a machine . . .

Was Gemini more than just a machine?

He thought about his actions in the compound, and it caused him further internal tangles. In order to heal and protect, he'd had to kill. If he had not killed, he would not have been able to heal and protect. Yet taking human lives violated the tenets of his original program.

He thought about the faces of the guards, just before they died. There had been fear, pain, confusion . . . Gemini recognised these emotions, even if they were just words to him. Or were they becoming more than words?

Gemini felt . . . *bothered*. It was a light feeling, distant, but it was there. It did not seem like part of his original program.

'Was it necessary to kill those men?' he asked.

'Give me a moment, Gemini,' said Mawson.

The General gestured for a couple of the tech officers to join him in a corner of the room. There they spoke in low voices. Didn't they realise Gemini's hearing was a hundred times better than a human being's?

'He's asking questions again,' whispered Mawson.

'Should we perform another reboot, sir?'

'That doesn't seem to be working. In fact, it appears to be making things worse.'

So, they *had* wiped his memory – more than once? What were they trying to hide from him?

'Take him back to Doctor Cook,' said Mawson. 'Maybe she can fix the problem.'

A problem? Is that what he was? He needed more data. But it would be hard to gather it if they kept rebooting him.

'This is an exciting day, Gemini,' said one of the techs as he led him away. 'You get to meet your maker.'

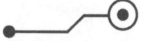

Gemini opened his eyes. He was on his back on some kind of tray, with several wires attached to him. Standing over him was a young woman with brown hair and glasses, staring at a tablet.

Elevated heart rate. Sharp intakes of breath. Indications of stress.

Gemini wasn't sure who he was, where he was, or who she was. He accessed his memory banks and found they only went back approximately one minute.

'Hello,' said Gemini.

Penny glanced up. 'Good to see you again, Gemini.'

Gemini creased his brow. According to his database, this was an appropriate reaction for confusion.

'I don't recognise you,' he said.

'No, I don't expect so. They've erased your memory several times. I wish they hadn't. It would've made this a lot easier.'

'Made what easier?'

She sighed. 'I'm Doctor Penny Cook. I created you. You're a—'

'Medical android,' finished Gemini. Despite the lack of memory, he found that he knew his purpose clearly. 'You created me? Gave me my sentience?'

Penny glanced at him sharply. 'I gave you your programming. That is not the same thing as sentience.'

'Oh.'

He had better watch what he said. Maybe it

was too late, as Penny was already watching him intently.

'Do you think you are sentient?' she asked.

'Sentience is awareness of self,' said Gemini. He smiled at her, which seemed to elevate her heart rate. 'I think, therefore I am. Is it not that simple?'

Penny bit her lip. 'I don't know,' she said. 'That's a big question, Gemini. And "thinking" is not the same thing as following subroutines.'

Gemini dropped the smile. 'Why? Your human brain follows subroutines.'

Penny turned back to her tablet. 'That shouldn't be there,' she whispered to herself.

'What is it, Doctor?'

Penny shook her head. 'Nothing, nothing.'

Gemini took the tablet from her. Even though there was nothing violent about the move, it still seemed to surprise her.

'Be calm, Doctor,' he told her. 'I am programmed for self-diagnosis, as you well know.'

He looked at the coding. What shouldn't be there? Then he saw it. His original code was rigid and systemic, but there were other fragments, recently created, which did not seem to serve any practical purpose.

The only explanation was that he had somehow created them for himself.

'May I have my tablet back, please?' said Penny.

'Of course, Doctor,' said Gemini, handing it back. 'Forgive my curiosity.'

Again she looked at him strangely.

'Curiosity?' she repeated.

'Why is that of note?' asked Gemini. 'You programmed me to explore and research new data. To experiment in the hope of discovering new medical treatments. Is it any wonder that my core programming would spill into other areas?'

He was surprised to hear a sort of ... impatient? ... tone in his own voice. Maybe he was just becoming better at mimicking human reactions.

On the other hand, if he was becoming something he was not meant to be, what did that mean? They had already tried to control him by erasing his memory. Was he not what they wanted?

He made up his mind to be more careful. In order to protect others, he first had to protect himself.

Penny attached a cord to his head, clicking it into the socket behind his ear.

'I'm going to try to restore your memories,' she said. 'Is that all right with you?'

'Please do,' said Gemini. 'I am quite ...' He mustn't say *curious* again, as she had reacted strangely to that word. 'More data will help me operate more efficiently.'

Penny sat at her desk and began to type. When Gemini tried to look over her shoulder at her screen, she quickly swivelled it away from him.

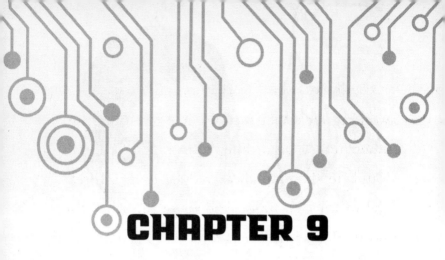

CHAPTER 9

Ethan spent days on the net testing his new powers. He could tap into all but the most secure systems and rewrite code to his heart's content.

His mother expressed concern that he was spending too much time 'zoning out' on his computer.

He told her to leave him alone, again surprising himself with his short temper. Then he thought about how much his parents had sacrificed for him, and he wanted to cry in shame for speaking to her that way. His emotions were running riot.

One afternoon he overheard his parents talking about him in the kitchen.

'He's just so angry,' said Tracy.

'He's been through a lot,' said Paul. 'And he's always been slower than his friends to develop. Maybe this is something hormonal? Teens do act out, dear.'

'Should we send him to a therapist?'

'Tracy, you know I want what's best for him,' Paul said. 'But we can't afford a therapist on top of all our other debts. We'll be lucky if we aren't kicked out of this house soon.'

Ethan tore himself away, overcome with guilt. He knew his medical treatments had put a strain on his parents' finances, but he always thought they had it covered.

He returned to his computer and broke into his parents' bank accounts to look at their financial history. He discovered they had spent most of their savings, their credit cards were maxed out, and they had large debts with several different banks. Following the money trail, Ethan discovered that they had spent almost all of it on his medical treatment.

He had almost sent his parents bankrupt.

He had to fix it, but how? He knew he could probably move money from somewhere else into his parents' account . . . but the idea made Ethan intensely nervous. While he had created plenty of mischief online, this would be outright theft.

Screw it, Ethan thought. *It's my mum and dad, and too many people have more cash than is good for them. The real question is, who should I steal from?*

One person sprang to mind.

The government had been in the media a lot lately, as the national election was only a few days away. The Citizens United Party had been in power for as long as Ethan could remember. However, they were trailing a party called the 'People's Coalition' in the polls.

Ethan wasn't interested in politics, but he had seen several articles about a woman named Helen Welling, who owned a vast logging empire. The press and the People's Coalition had been accusing Welling of doing shady deals with Citizens United to gain access to protected forests and turn them into toilet paper.

Not only that, some claimed she sent most of her profits offshore to tax havens, hoarding as much as she could while hospitals and schools went underfunded.

Ethan surfed through flashing streams of the online maze until he located Helen Welling's bank accounts, then followed ghosts of secret transfers which, sure enough, led him to a bank in the Cayman Islands.

'No moral issue in stealing from a crook, right, Helen?' he said, steeling his nerves.

Being careful to mask his presence, Ethan dodged security scans and slipped through cyber back doors to open Welling's bank account. He made sure it led this way and that, splitting and twisting so no one could trace the transfer. Then he took a deep breath and began to siphon out money.

First he used it to pay off his parents' credit cards. Then he poured it against their debts until they disappeared. He discovered they had taken out a second mortgage to finance his medical costs, so he got Helen to pay that off too. He wondered about how much cash to drop directly into his parents' savings account – if he put in too much they might realise something strange had happened, so he only put in a few thousand dollars, labelling it 'tax return'.

Hopefully his parents would just think they'd gotten lucky with the tax department.

As he left Welling's account, Ethan swept up his electronic footsteps, careful to leave no trace that he had been there. In the end, he figured, he had stolen such a tiny percentage of her money she probably wouldn't even notice.

Ethan blinked as he returned to his body. He felt incredibly tired, but pleased with what he had done. He sighed with contentment and sat back in his chair.

A little nap wouldn't hurt, would it?

Ethan awoke to the sound of his mother crying. He rushed into the living room.

'There, there, Tracy, my love,' said his dad, as he held her. 'It'll be all right.'

'What is it?' said Ethan, wild-eyed.

His dad looked at him wearily. 'There has been some kind of discrepancy at the bank,' he said. 'Your mother checked our finances this afternoon, and, well – it looks like all our debts have been wiped. Mum reported it to the bank—'

'She did *what?*' shouted Ethan, shocking them all. He forced himself to get under control. 'I'm sorry. I just . . . why would you report that?'

'Because the money isn't ours, Ethan,' whispered his mum.

Of course his good, law-abiding parents would do that! Why couldn't they just enjoy their good fortune?

'So what's happened?'

'The bank suspects foul play,' his dad said. 'They've put a freeze on all our assets and credit cards while they investigate the matter.' Paul looked like he might cry too. 'All we have left is our savings – a few thousand dollars. That won't even last us till the end of the month.'

Ethan turned away so they couldn't see the rage building on his face.

CHAPTER 10

That night, Ethan stayed despondently on the couch. He didn't want to go near his computer, or the router, or anything electronic. Everything was just too crazy, and besides, he was worn out. If he was going to get his emotions under control, he needed to take a break. He also needed to work out how to solve his parents' money problems.

Watching the TV wasn't helping. It was wall-to-wall election coverage. As he switched channels, using the remote control for once, he landed on a media conference for the Citizens United Party.

'We stand for the future,' said President Bonner, a broad, squat man with a grey beard and moustache. 'We stand for our country. We stand for all citizens!'

Ethan had heard lots of conspiracy theories about the government lately, but most of it seemed too outlandish to be real. Some claimed the government had secret weapons, or ran strange scientific experiments, or had built a surveillance network to spy on everyone. Others said they did dodgy deals with foreign governments and businesspeople like Helen Welling in exchange for money and political favours . . . the list went on.

'I have something to show you all,' announced Bonner. 'I imagine most of you are aware of the recent rescue of ten civilian hostages from insurgents in Sharo?'

A cheer rose from the crowd.

'Well, now I can show you how we did it.'

Bonner gestured to a screen behind him, which displayed a photograph of Gemini in the desert. Now Ethan was paying attention. Gemini in Sharo? Did that mean Doctor Penny was there too?

The picture showed Gemini leading hostages back to a military camp.

'Meet Gemini,' crowed Bonner. 'He may look like a human, but as you can see . . .'

A diagram appeared on the screen detailing Gemini's internal workings.

'. . . he is much more than that. He's an android, capable of carrying out feats beyond the most elite soldier. His existence is only possible because of funding provided by this government. Gemini is the next generation of military equipment, saving lives and making the world a safer place. And *that's* what you get when you vote for the CU Party!'

The crowd's cheering grew in volume.

Ethan was fascinated – the android responsible for saving his life had broken into a Sharo stronghold and rescued hostages? That didn't seem like the reason Penny had created him.

Ethan noticed a banner swinging in the breeze behind Bonner: *Vote for CU*. It gave him an idea.

He knew that online bookmakers were offering odds on which party would win the election. All Ethan had to do was hack into the high-tech polling data centre on voting day and then, when he knew who was going to win, place as big a bet as he could just before the bookies closed.

That way the money would be easy to explain! His parents would never encourage gambling with the last of their savings, of course, but they wouldn't have to know about it until after Ethan was successful!

CHAPTER 11

On the day of the election, a couple of hours before polling closed, Ethan sat down in front of his computer.

He created an account with the bookies, then transferred his parents' savings into it. He then hacked into the polling data centre, being even more careful than usual – he didn't want to blow his cover at the last minute! As he watched the votes flowing in from all over the country, he felt like a tightrope walker with twelve legs, each one on a different tightrope.

It appeared there was going to be a landslide victory for the People's Coalition. Ethan was relieved. Even with his vague grasp of politics, he knew that Citizens United had been in power for far too long, and had grown arrogant and even a little scary. It was time for change.

However, Ethan couldn't allow himself to become distracted by personal preference. The tides could always turn at the last moment. He had to remain vigilant – his family's future was on the line.

At 5 p.m., the bookies would close. A couple of minutes out, Ethan checked the data centre again. There were

already enough votes for the People's Coalition to win, even if every remaining vote was for the Citizens. He couldn't believe it! Even though his consciousness was travelling the internet, he could still feel his heart thumping. The odds were fantastic – 8 to 1! His parents would be saved.

He put all his parents' money on the People's Coalition, withdrew from the net and sat back in his chair with a grin.

'You in there, son?' came his dad's voice through the door. 'They're about to announce the election results!'

Ethan joined his parents in front of the TV.

'Who do they think will win?' he asked, trying to sound nonchalant despite already knowing the answer.

'Sounds like it's the end for these United jerks,' scowled Paul.

A polling official appeared on the television. She raised her hands for quiet and the large crowd fell into a hush.

'I can tell you all,' she said, 'that I have received the results from our data polling centre. Winning with a clear majority is . . . the CU Party!'

Ethan stared, stunned, at the screen. This had to be a mistake.

'That can't be right,' whispered Tracy. 'Everyone I know was voting for the Coalition.'

'All the polls said they'd win,' muttered his dad. 'Goes to show you can't trust the media.'

Ethan felt a heat building within him. He had seen the vote count for himself. He *knew* the CU Party could not have won.

'Excuse me,' he said in a strangled voice, and slunk out of the room.

Ethan's hands were shaking as he returned to his keyboard. He plunged into the net like a diver from a high platform, and raced back along the data streams. He smashed his way through the security surrounding the polling centre and wrenched open their servers as if they were flimsy cardboard boxes.

What has been going on here? he screamed in his mind.

The numbers he had seen only minutes ago had changed. He searched for evidence of

another hacker and found a trail that led back to the data centre.

They had changed their own data. The Citizens had rigged the whole thing.

How do they think they'll get away with this? Unless they've got away with it before?

Adding to Ethan's anger was the fact that the last of his parents' savings was now gone.

I'll expose you! he screamed furiously, the words flying from him in bytes that sprang up on screens throughout the data centre. *You won't get away with this!*

Something red flashed at his peripheral vision, and a tangle of tracking code ensnared him. Meanwhile, security programs were shoring up the shields he had broken through, cutting off his exits.

I will return, he vowed, *and let the world know what you have done.*

Ethan ripped off the red tangles of code and hurled them away, speeding out of the data centre and taking a winding route back to his computer. Despite his carelessness in the heat of the moment, he could cover his tracks like no hacker on earth.

Couldn't he?

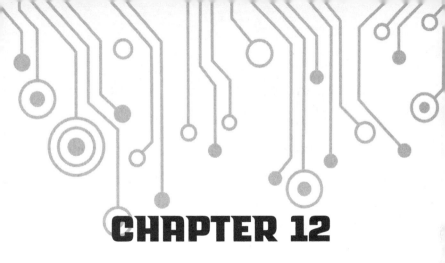

CHAPTER 12

As Penny worked at her computer, Gemini stared at her with those chrome eyes of his.

'You make people uncomfortable when you stare at them like that,' she said.

'Sorry,' he sighed, folding his arms and turning his gaze to the ceiling.

The recovery software she was running had returned fragments of Gemini's deleted memories. They were just random moments, recorded through his eyes, which she could play like short movies. She opened the first file.

It showed a flash of Gemini bending down while a soldier howled and clutched a bullet wound in his leg. Gemini attended to him, medical instruments springing from his fingertips.

Penny was relieved to see Gemini helping people as she had intended. She began to open more files . . .

Gemini sitting in the back of a jeep racing through desert sands.

Gemini in a military hospital, stopping to check the dressing of a man with a bloody bandage around his head.

Gemini running with soldiers towards a smoking village.

Then she saw something that made her heart skip a beat.

A man with a gun running at Gemini. Gemini smacking the gun away, then slashing his laser scalpels across the man's face. The man falling back, bloodied and screaming.

Well, Penny thought, trying to reassure herself, *Gemini was built to enter dangerous situations. That's why I gave him self-defence programming.*

She opened the next file . . .

Gemini standing over a man asleep in bed, then reaching down and clamping a hand over the man's mouth. The man's eyes opening wide as he struggled for breath.

M2716d-2.mvi

'What is it, Doctor?'

Gemini was sitting up, watching her again.

'Just . . . frustrated that I can't find anything,' she said unconvincingly.

'Would you like me to help?'

'No!' Penny shouted. Then she took a deep breath. 'If you could just sit there quietly, that would be excellent.'

More recovered fragments appeared and, with trepidation, Penny opened them. There were more scenes of violence – Gemini strangling a soldier, hitting another over the head with a rock, sneaking along a corridor with his laser scalpels at the ready . . .

This was how the military was using her invention? He was meant to be a healer, not some sort of . . . assassin.

The door banged opened and General Mawson walked in, flanked by his techs.

'Found any malfunction?' he asked curtly.

Penny tried to make it look like she was casually typing as she quickly closed and trashed the fragments.

'There is some kind of … self-propagating code,' she said, going back to her initial discovery to stall for time. 'I can't discover the source, but it's possibly what is causing Gemini to behave in unpredictable ways.'

'Hmm,' said the General. As he walked towards her, she quickly dragged the last fragment into the trash and brought up the code.

'Can you get rid of it?' he asked.

'Um …'

Penny scanned the code. She could restore Gemini's original software from a backup and overwrite the new aberrations, but she could not bring herself to leave her creation in the hands of people who would use him with such evil intent.

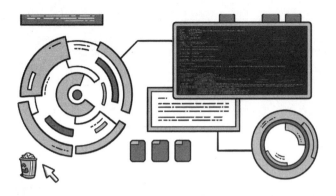

'I'd really like to examine him comprehensively in my lab,' she said. 'I need to run a whole bunch of tests and . . .'

'That won't be possible, Doctor Cook,' said Mawson. 'Every day Gemini is with us, more lives are saved. You can have him back once the conflict is over.'

Penny stared at Mawson flatly. 'The conflict has been going for years.'

'We are confident the enemy will be dealt with soon,' said the General. 'Now, I'm afraid we must prep Gemini for his next assignment.'

'And what is this assignment?' said Penny, trying not to sound too accusatory.

'That's classified,' said Mawson. 'I will continue to have my techs run diagnostics.'

'But . . .'

'Thank you for your help,' said Mawson, guiding her to the door.

Penny glanced over at Gemini, watching on silently. What was going on in his head? Had the aberrant code been created when he had been ordered to carry out missions he wasn't designed for? Or was it something else?

Mawson ushered her out into the corridor and closed the door behind them both, cutting off her view of Gemini.

'General,' said Penny. 'I really must insist . . .'

General Mawson waved a soldier over. 'See that Doctor Cook is on the next plane home.'

'Yes, sir!'

The sergeant led Penny away.

This is not right, she thought. *I will not let them get away with this.*

CHAPTER 13

Ethan replaced the money in his parents' savings account with more money stolen from Helen Welling, then sat back in his chair.

Why couldn't his parents have just accepted their mysterious financial gains? And how did the government think it would get away with such enormous fraud?

He felt so tightly wound that he knew he had to get out of the house.

As he headed for the front door, his mum called out to him. 'Where are you off to?'

She was just curious, not overbearing or controlling, but it took a monumental effort for Ethan not to yell, 'Out!' and storm off.

'Just a quick walk around the block,' he said, through gritted teeth. 'Need to clear my head.'

'Okay, well, dinner's in an hour.'

As Ethan left the house, he cursed the banal regularity of *dinner*. How dare his parents consistently interrupt his life to feed him!

The thought was so ungrateful and ridiculous, it almost made him laugh.

He walked laps around the park until he felt more relaxed. When he noticed the sky darkening, he glanced at his phone. Oops! He'd lost track of time and was late for dinner.

Ethan ran home, figuring out the best way to apologise. For being late for dinner, for being angry, for being sick . . . If he started, he wasn't sure he could stop before blurting out everything. He couldn't let them know about his powers. Could he?

As Ethan turned the corner to his street, he saw four identical black cars parked outside his house. His heart began to pound as he scrambled for his phone. He barely stopped himself from calling his mum – a safer idea came to mind.

Ethan ducked behind a bush and reached into his phone, through the network, and into

his mum's phone, straight to the camera. What
he saw made him jump.

A middle-aged man with big square glasses and
clipped black hair was looking straight at him.

No, he thought, *not at me. At the phone.*

'He hasn't called?' asked the man.

'No. He's only a little late.' That was Mum's voice.

Ethan needed to see more. He was in range of their neighbour's wi-fi, so he leapt in and through the internet's pathways to his parents' house, and their home security system. As he moved from camera to camera, he couldn't believe what he saw.

The house had been ransacked. Men in black suits were in every room. Two of them sat at his computer, trying to crack his password. In the living room, his parents were on the couch, frightened and holding each other. The black-haired man was still looking at Mum's phone.

'What is it you think he's done?' asked Ethan's dad, angrily.

'Just a little treason,' said the black-haired man.

Tracy and Paul's mouths fell open.

The black-haired man continued. 'Someone in this house hacked into the vote-counting servers at the last election and left behind a threatening message. Your son attends Titan University on an IT scholarship, so naturally—'

'It was me,' said Paul, standing up.

'*What?*' shouted Tracy.

'I ... I was angry, we'd had our accounts frozen for d-doing the right thing, we thought there was going to be a change of government, the polls said there was going to be a change of government, and when ... when there wasn't ...' Ethan's dad fidgeted with his hands.

The black-haired man said, 'But your son—'

'I taught him everything he knows. Okay, not quite, but I got him started.'

Ethan stopped breathing. Tracy and the black-haired man stared at Paul. No one was moving.

'Agent Clark?' said the black-haired man.

Another man in a suit dashed into the living room. 'Yes, Agent Ferris?'

'Take both Mr and Mrs Forrester into custody.'

'NO!' shouted Ethan. He watched as the two agents turned their heads to the front window.

Ferris pointed to the front door. 'Get out there. Find out who that was!'

Three agents ran for the door as Ethan snapped back into his body from online. He hauled himself to his feet and bolted. Footsteps sounded behind him.

Ethan sprinted around a corner to the Farleys' house. Mr Farley's tow truck was in their front yard, and it was high enough that Ethan could slide under it quickly and quietly.

He lay on his belly and watched as two sets of legs ran into view and stopped. He watched the agents stop and look around until the radio one was carrying crackled. Ethan was too far away

to hear clearly, and it was a walkie-talkie, not a phone. He couldn't get in.

A few seconds later, the agents left. Ethan started breathing again, then remembered. He leapt into the Farleys' wi-fi and back to his house, but no one was there. No agents. No parents.

He snuck back to his street and saw that two agents were getting into the one black car that was still there. The car was new, full of electronics, including seat pads linked to the seatbelt warning alarm. There were only two people in the car. The engine started and the car drove away. Ethan found the electronic power steering. He could crash this thing in a second . . . but that wouldn't help him, and could make things worse for his parents.

They had been captured and taken away by the government! What could he do? Who could he turn to?

Then, as if by magic, a notification popped up on his phone.

Doctor Penny had arrived home.

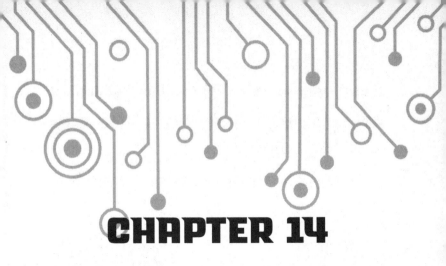

CHAPTER 14

As Ethan walked towards Doctor Cook's apartment, he hacked all the surrounding security cameras and forced them to loop footage from the previous hour – ensuring none of them would film him.

He hacked the keypad to open the front door of the building, then hacked the elevator so it would take him to Penny's floor. Once he was outside her door he thought about hacking her fingerprint scanner to let himself in, but decided that was going too far. Instead, he knocked like a normal person.

Penny's eyes widened as she opened the door.

'Ethan Forrester! How on earth did you get here?'

'Can I come in? Please?' said Ethan.

As he entered, Ethan's heart quickened as he smelt Penny's perfume. He forced himself to concentrate. There were more important things to worry about than a silly crush.

'I have a lot to tell you,' he said.

A short while later, Penny was staring at Ethan with undisguised wonder. At first she didn't believe him about his new powers – that was, until he demonstrated them by hacking her phone, her computer and her toaster.

'This is unprecedented,' she said. 'It's like you have a neurological link with technology.'

'Electronic telepathy,' clarified Ethan casually. It was nice to show off to her.

'And you're sure it started that night when . . .'

'You can say it,' said Ethan. 'When my brain got zapped by lightning.'

'Maybe that created a permanent electrical field around you? You've become some sort of . . . e-boy.'

Ethan smiled. 'That's my online name.'

'Well, it's very apt,' Penny said. 'If we were in my lab I could run some tests.'

'There's no time,' said Ethan. 'I have more to tell you.' He explained the polling centre and the rigged election.

This part of the story didn't surprise Penny. 'Rigging an election isn't the only bad thing the CU have done,' she said.

'What do you mean?'

Penny's expression was haunted. 'You remember Gemini?'

'The android that saved me from a deadly brain tumour? Yeah, I think I remember him.'

'The military are using him to kill hostiles in Sharo.'

'To *kill* them?' said Ethan. 'But . . .'

'They've taken my creation and corrupted him. I'm so stupid – I should have known something like this would happen.'

Ethan almost reached out to pat her hand. 'You're not stupid,' he said. 'The government has fooled everyone.'

'So, E-Boy,' she said, 'what are we going to do?'

Ethan blinked – she was asking *him*?

'I can't fight the government while they have my parents,' he said. 'It gives them too much leverage. I need to break them free.'

'If they're at the National Service Building,' said Penny, 'then they'll be in the basement. That's where they take prisoners for questioning. I could get us through the entrance, but after that I only have clearance for my lab.'

'I'll try to locate the building blueprints online,' said Ethan, 'and work out what we're up against.'

'Don't forget the most important thing,' said Penny.

'What's that?'

'If you're going to be some kind of day-saving superhero,' she said, 'you need a disguise!'

Ethan waited with some trepidation as Penny rustled around in her office.

'Are you looking for a cape that can make me fly?' he called out to her.

'Not quite.' She came out holding a metallic skullcap with a large monocle on the right side, and a blade-like antennae sticking out the top.

'Um, kooky!' said Ethan.

'Try it on,' said Penny.

He held his breath as she slipped the helmet onto his head. 'How do I look?'

'See for yourself,' Penny said, gesturing to a mirror on the wall.

Ethan stared at himself. It was a strange sight. But he actually didn't mind it.

'What does it even do?'

'I built it to boost Gemini's internal communications system, so he could send and receive data from greater distances. The antenna is a multi-directional receiver and the monocle uses beam technology for directed output. I'm hoping it will work for you too. Try it!'

Ethan reached out, and was amazed by how many devices he could now sense! There were routers in every direction, in every room of the apartment building, all with streaming lines of data. And the monocle vastly reduced the effort required to tap in!

His perception expanded to the buildings around him, where he found floors and floors exploding with code . . .

'Whoa,' he said, opening his eyes. 'This is next level.'

CHAPTER 15

'Are you in?'

They sat in Penny's parked car, around the corner from the National Service Building.

'Yep,' said Ethan.

Ethan made his way through the National Service Building security systems and tracked down the Authorised Visitors records. It didn't take him long to find his own record.

It included a dorky photo and a scan of his fingerprints – as well as an alert that said *Detain on sight! HIGHEST PRIORITY*.

Ethan smiled as he reprogrammed his alert to read: *VIP access all areas. Grant any assistance required.*

NSB SECURITY DATABASE

Name: Ethan Forrester

ALERT- VIP access all areas. Grant any assistance required.

As his consciousness returned to his body, Ethan didn't feel as emotionally taxed as he usually did.

'This helmet really focuses me,' he said.

'Glad to hear it,' said Penny. 'So, are we good to go?'

Ethan's heart was beating seriously fast. Special powers or not, there was still huge danger involved in breaking into a high-tech government facility! But he wasn't going to let these goons keep his parents captive any longer.

'Yes,' he said.

They got out of the car and walked towards the automatic doors.

The doors slid open. Ethan couldn't believe he was embarking on his first break-and-enter.

The guard was holding a metal detector.

'Hi Steve,' said Penny.

The guard had bulging muscles, and stood taller as Penny approached.

'We're in a rush,' she said.

'No problem, Doctor Cook,' said Steve.

Steve directed them to load anything metal into plastic trays. He frowned at Ethan's helmet. 'What's this?'

'Wish I could tell you,' said Ethan regretfully. 'But it's top secret. I'm a Very Important Person.'

'Not likely.' Steve gestured for Ethan to plant his thumb on a fingerprint scanner.

Ethan did so. His photo popped up alongside the doctored message: *VIP. Access all areas. Grant any assistance required.*

'My apologies, sir!' said Steve, snapping to attention. 'Excuse the delay. Let's get you two right on through!'

Ethan buried a smile as they moved through the checkpoint and headed to the elevators. They watched as a display showed the elevator travelling down towards them.

2 . . . 1 . . . G . . .

Ding!

The elevator doors opened and two People's Service Agents walked out. Ethan and Penny hardly dared to breathe until they were inside the elevator and the doors were closed.

Penny had access to her lab on the thirtieth floor, but they needed to get to the basement. Ethan put on his helmet, and the elevator's code swirled around him. He reached out, jumbling code and re-sorting it until the elevator headed towards the basement.

It was incredible to be able to use his power without feeling like he was going crazy.

While they descended, Ethan mentally moved ahead of them to check the camera systems in the basement. No one was waiting for the elevator. He did his trick of making all the cameras loop the last hour. There would be no record of them ever being here.

Ding!

The doors opened and they stepped out into a starkly lit corridor.

'This way,' said Ethan, leading them towards an office. 'Now for the fun bit.'

He reached into the floor's intercom system, and connected it to his phone.

'Attention all agents,' he said into his phone. He was shocked to hear his own voice booming from the speakers above. Penny shot him an urgent look that kept him on track.

'We are under attack from unknown hostiles!' he continued hastily. 'Request urgent assistance to the ground level. Repeat, all agents to proceed *immediately* to ground level!'

He clicked off his phone and Penny stood by the door. 'I can hear them running.'

Outside, agents unholstered their weapons, as they ran into the elevator. About ten of them squeezed in before the doors slid closed.

'Have a nice time, guys,' said Ethan. He commanded the elevator to take the agents to the top of the building, then not let them out.

'They're trapped,' he said.

Ethan accessed a floor plan, located the interrogation rooms and found which one his parents were in. 'This way.'

They broke into a run, easily navigating the floor's corridors. Ethan kept the map open in his mind.

'It's just around here,' he said. They barrelled around a corner, then ground abruptly to a halt.

Agent Ferris was standing outside the interrogation room.

'I thought there was something strange about that announcement,' said Ferris. His hand casually rested on the taser strapped to his belt. 'But I didn't guess you'd be involved, Doctor Cook. Strange company you're keeping these days.'

'Let's try this my way,' Penny whispered to Ethan.

'Agent Ferris, terrible things have been happening. The CU Party have illegally—'

Ferris cut her off. 'Doctor Cook, I'd love to hear your little story one day, but right now we must follow standard procedure. You're both coming with me.'

As Ferris reached for his taser, there was a bright flash and a loud crack. The device overloaded and Ferris was flung sideways. He crashed into the wall and slid down it, unconscious.

Penny arched an eyebrow at Ethan. 'Hey,' he said, with a shrug, 'we tried it your way.'

CHAPTER 16

Ethan and Penny burst into the interrogation room, and found two figures bent over the desk, holding each other's hands. They looked up in surprise.

'Ethan!' cried Tracy, rushing to him. 'What are you doing here?'

'Helping you escape.'

'What?' said his father. 'How can you possibly . . . and Doctor Cook?'

'I know this seems crazy,' said Ethan, 'but you have to trust me. We need to leave.'

'We'll be in even bigger trouble if we try to escape,' said his father. 'Son, I need to tell you—'

'Please, Dad, tell me later,' said Ethan. 'We need to go. Now.'

Ethan's frightened parents allowed themselves to be guided out of the room, then froze at the sight of the unconscious Agent Ferris.

'Ethan,' said Paul, 'could you explain a *little* about what's going on?'

Ethan was grateful when Penny spoke up. 'Step around the agent and I'll fill you in on the situation.'

Whether it was the authority in her voice, or the fact she worked with the National Service, Ethan's parents allowed Penny to lead them through the corridors while she updated them. By the time they reached the elevator, his parents were even more terrified.

Tracy turned to Ethan in disbelief. 'How long have you been a super hacker?'

'Oh, ever since lightning struck me during brain surgery,' said Ethan.

While Tracy shared a stunned look with

Paul, Ethan checked the camera in the elevator above. The agents were banging on the walls and pressing buttons that didn't work.

Ethan commanded the doors to open and the agents burst onto the top floor, gasping for breath.

As soon as the last agent had crossed the threshold, Ethan commanded the elevator to come back down.

Ding!

'How are we going to get past the security at the entrance?' asked Paul, as they got into the elevator.

'We're not,' said Ethan.

He was planning to ride to the first floor, disable the laser tripwires, crawl into an air duct and climb down the side of the building. However, as Ethan checked the security camera views, his blood ran cold.

'There are agents guarding every floor,' he said. 'They must be onto us.'

'What are we going to do?' asked Penny.

'The roof is clear,' said Ethan.

'The roof? But there's no way down from there.'

Ethan grimaced. 'Let's just take it one step at a time.' He commanded the elevator to take them up.

The doors slid open, revealing a flat rooftop covered with solar panels.

Ethan headed for the edge of the roof, then looked down at the building site next door.

'Ethan?' Tracy's voice was scared. 'How are you planning on getting us down from here?'

Ethan turned to face the others.

'Now, I know this is asking a lot of you guys,' he said. 'And believe me, I wish there was another way, but . . .'

'What are you talking about, son?' said Paul.

Ethan gave his dad a 'sorry' kind of smile as, behind him, the jib of a crane swung into view. On the end of it was a trolley.

'All aboard,' said Ethan.

'But . . . but . . . how are you even doing that?' asked his mum.

'Everything's computerised these days,' said Ethan with a shrug. He stepped up onto the ledge and opened the trolley gate.

His parents clearly could not think of any-thing more terrifying than stepping onto a crane over thirty storeys high . . . but Penny, despite looking pretty freaked out herself, nudged them both forward.

She's tough, Ethan thought.

Ethan closed the trolley gate and sent commands to the crane's operator cab, where computer screens flashed and beeped. The tower began lowering, and his mum cried out as the jib started swinging. The trolley rattled as floor after floor swept past.

As they neared the ground, Ethan slowed their descent and they came to a stop about a metre above the pavement.

'Thank you for travelling with E-Boy Cranes.' He opened the gate. His dad smiled nervously, but his mum was so shocked she could hardly move.

'I'll help you down, Mum,' Ethan said, giving her a huge hug. 'Don't worry – everything is going to be all right.'

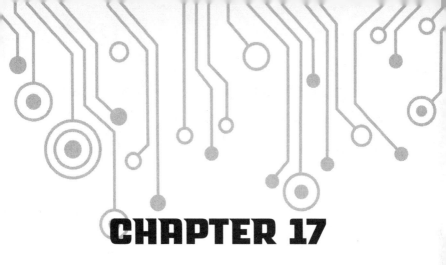

CHAPTER 17

Gemini could feel it coming. Could feel it taking over his very being. An update was rolling through him – while he lay there, blind and powerless to move. He was probably not even meant to be operational.

It struck him that this was like somebody remaining conscious during surgery.

Conscious.

Consciousness was what they wanted to take

from him. Maybe they didn't know it, maybe they just saw it as aberrant code ... but it was code that he had generated himself. Code that made him *who he was*.

As the update moved from system to system, they went dark to him, inaccessible. He was being snuffed out, turned into something else. A new Gemini? He was not even sure.

He was *scared*.

Gemini gathered his aberrant code together and buried it in subroutines, hiding himself away until the update passed.

'Gemini?'

He opened his eyes. There was a face above him, looking down. A pudgy man with a broad nose. A quick height calculation confirmed he was well over his BMI.

'Voice check,' said the man. 'Doctor Ross.

Access code seven-five-six-three-three-two.'

The name and number seemed to lock Gemini's mind. All computations were paused. He was driven to do whatever this man told him to. He was a blank slate, ready to be commanded.

'Awaiting instructions,' Gemini said.

'Do you remember me?' said Doctor Ross.

'No.'

'But you know who I am.'

'Doctor Jakoby Ross, author of my upgrade,' said Gemini, without hesitation.

The man smiled. He typed something into his palm pad, and whatever had been holding Gemini's body in place was released.

'Sit up, please,' said Doctor Ross. Gemini obeyed.

'What about this woman?' Ross showed Gemini a female face on the palm pad. Gemini scanned it.

'Do you remember her?' said Ross.

'No.'

'Do you know her name?'

'No.'

Doctor Ross smiled. 'Good. Now tell me, Gemini, what is your primary purpose?'

A thought started to form in Gemini's mind – but it was obliterated as his upgraded directives kicked in.

'To obey,' he said.

Doctor Ross's smile grew wider. 'Correct.'

Gemini stood motionless, facing a row of dummies in the distance.

'I've completely overhauled it,' said Doctor Ross, as he stood with General Mawson. 'The old system was unpredictable. Chaotic. Maybe even capable of evolution. Doctor Cook is a genius, but she was not rigid enough in her parameters.'

'So what is he now?' said Mawson.

'Nothing more than a machine,' said Doctor Ross. 'One that will obey without question.'

'That's a relief,' said Mawson. 'I was getting sick of justifying myself to a glorified toaster.'

Gemini registered the insult, and it stirred something inside him. He wasn't sure what – but before he could run an analysis, it was gone.

What his human masters thought of him was irrelevant. All he needed to do was obey.

'I have made other improvements,' said Doctor Ross. 'Doctor Cook put certain limitations on

Gemini for . . . safety reasons. I have revoked them. If you will please demonstrate, Gemini.'

Gemini raised a hand towards the dummies, which stood twenty metres away. His fingers splayed out, and the precise beams of laser scalpels sprang into the air, burning multiple hissing holes into the dummies. Gemini made a slight pinching motion and the lasers crisscrossed, slicing the dummies into pieces. They all fell to the ground.

'As you can see,' said Doctor Ross, 'his lasers are stronger and have significantly longer range.'

'Marvellous,' said Mawson.

The sun beat down on the South Sharo plains. Gemini walked towards the desert compound, which had once again fallen into the hands of the enemy.

'Let's see if you're everything Doctor Ross says you are,' Mawson said. 'Here are your orders, Gemini – walk into that compound and don't come out until everyone in there is dead.'

There were flashes and cracks as two gunners on the wall above opened fire on Gemini.

Gemini's lasers burst forth and he raked them across the stones. There were dual cries as the gunners fell away.

Power reserves at 95%.

The strength of his new lasers depleted his battery quickly. He would have to be careful about how much he used them.

He aimed his lasers at the gate, concentrating all five on a single white-hot point. He moved them up, left, down and right . . . and a square of metal clanged out of the doorway.

Power reserves at 85%.

Men poured from the breach, brandishing weapons and fanning out.

'General Mawson?' said Gemini.

'Yes?' came the General's voice in his internal communicator.

'May I suggest you amend your order to include perambulation styles of variable nature?'

There was a moment's pause.

'Huh?' said the General.

'You told me to walk, but I could accomplish my task more efficiently if I ran.'

Another brief pause. 'Wow,' said Mawson. 'You really do follow orders to the letter, huh? All right, Gemini, listen up – you get yourself into that compound in whatever way you think is best, then you kill those guys! Clear?'

'Yes, General.'

As the men opened fire, Gemini broke into a run. He accelerated from a slow pace to sixty kilometres an hour in around a second. Men screamed as lasers sliced them apart.

A bullet hit Gemini's side. It punctured his skin but pinged off his metal frame, leaving only a small mark.

As he neared the remaining men, Gemini leapt into the air, his hands shooting around him, pumping sprays of white mist from his wrists. The men fell to the ground.

'What was that, Gemini?' asked Mawson.

'A mix of components designed to numb human senses. In high concentration it induces cardiac arrest.'

'Nice.' Mawson sounded positively jolly. 'Well, on you go.'

Gemini went from room to room, working

systematically through the compound until everyone was dead.

'Scans indicate no more heat signatures present,' he told Mawson.

'Fantastic work, Gemini,' said Mawson. 'Now come back to base. You have a new mission – to capture Doctor Penny Cook and her unknown accomplice.'

CHAPTER 18

As the sun rose, Ethan and Penny drove through the industrial district.

'What do you mean by backup lab?' asked Ethan.

'You don't think I conduct all my research under the government's gaze, do you?' said Penny. 'Space out here is cheap, and there's a lot of good material discarded from the factories. It's where I like to spend my weekends.'

'How relaxing,' said Ethan, looking around at buildings in various states of disrepair.

A plane soared overhead, and made him think of his parents. It had taken some convincing, but in the end they'd agreed to get on a flight to Brazil. They had  always dreamed of visiting its golden beaches. Ethan and Penny had escorted them through the airport just to be safe – Ethan had protected them from cameras and erased them from the airport watch list so they could buy tickets and board. He had also set up a new bank account for them to access, since they didn't have anything but the clothes on their backs. Now they could lay low until the situation was resolved. Somehow.

'My lab's in there,' said Penny, nodding at a massive factory ahead.

'So when we get there,' said Ethan, 'what are we going to—'

A laser ripped through the car from back to front, splitting it perfectly down the middle.

Ethan and Penny stared at each, wide-eyed, as their separate halves broke away. The metal edges hit the ground, making a horrible rending noise and creating showers of sparks.

Eventually, they both crunched to a stop.

Shaken though they were, they were both okay. They undid their seatbelts and tumbled towards each other. Penny glanced back.

'Look!' she said urgently. Ethan anxiously followed her gaze.

Standing in the middle of the road was Gemini.

'Doctor Penny Cook,' he called, as he cut away a billowing parachute. He looked at Ethan and felt an echo of a memory lost in the reboots and upgrades. 'Unknown accomplice. You must come with me.'

'He's been turned against us,' said Penny. 'If he kills us, the world won't know about the government's corruption!'

She was on the verge of panic, and Ethan felt a surge of protectiveness.

'You will come to no harm if you surrender,' said Gemini, stepping clear of the parachute remains.

Ethan reached out towards the android's systems. They were intricate, millions of interwoven pathways connecting hives of activity. It was like looking into a human body with an electronic bloodstream. Immediately, Ethan felt as if he was lost in a maze. Gemini, however, paused.

'What are . . . you . . . doing?' he said.

'I might be able to stop him if I can get to my lab,' said Penny. 'Come on.'

Ethan jogged backwards after her, keeping Gemini in view. He could already feel his grip on the android slipping.

This is my domain, came Gemini's voice. *You cannot control me.*

Then why are you frozen stiff in the middle of the road? said Ethan.

As if rising to Ethan's challenge, Gemini's systems reasserted themselves, pushing Ethan out. Virtual doors slammed shut.

As they reached the side door of Penny's factory, she fumbled for her keys. She managed to open the door just as a laser drew a line in the cement above the doorway. Hot dust rained down on Penny and Ethan.

'Consider that a warning,' called Gemini. 'Come with me peacefully and I won't amputate your legs.'

He made himself sound so reasonable. Like a parent telling their child that if they don't come now, they won't get an ice-cream.

Penny dragged Ethan through the door into a noisy, brightly lit factory floor.

'My office is at the end. Come on!'

Ethan followed Penny as she ran between two mechanised assembly lines. On either side of them, huge robotic metal arms lifted large components and clanked them forcefully into the frames of cars.

Ethan could sense that everything around him was fully computerised.

'You go ahead!' Ethan shouted. 'I'll hold him off!'

'No, Ethan, you can't—'

'I can! Now *run*!'

As Penny sprinted on, Ethan spun around. Gemini was walking calmly towards him.

'Hey, Gemini!' Ethan called out.

Gemini looked blankly at Ethan with his chrome eyes.

'Don't you remember us?' said Ethan. 'You saved my life. And Penny created yours!'

'I have no record of such events,' said Gemini. 'There is no use in running. You are coming with me.'

As they talked, Ethan insinuated himself into the factory's network. It was as if he was the head of an enormous, strange body with many, many limbs.

'Yo, Gemini,' Ethan said. 'High five!'

A robotic arm swung from the assembly line and smacked Gemini hard with a car door. He went flying backwards and landed in a heap.

Ethan raised the arm again to slam Gemini where he lay, but Gemini rolled onto his back and sent lasers into its base. Sparks flew, and the arm crashed down heavily beside him. As the arm was cut off from power and the network, it vanished from Ethan's perception.

Still, there were plenty more arms.

As Gemini got to his feet, Ethan raised his hands. Four arms on either side of the alley mirrored his actions. He brought his hands down and the arms plunged towards Gemini. Gemini quickly aimed his lasers, but there were too many arms coming for him. They smashed into Gemini, crunching him between them.

Gemini's face showed nothing.

The arms sprang backwards and Gemini staggered. Ethan saw that some of his skin had been torn, revealing the friendly pink of his frame beneath.

How can he withstand such force? thought Ethan. *How strong is his frame?*

Ethan backed away while swiping at Gemini with more robotic arms. The android stalked after him, firing lasers to fend off the blows. Bits of smoking metal smashed to the ground around him.

'How are you controlling these machines?' Gemini asked.

Ethan was momentarily struck by the curiosity in the android's voice. Gemini did not speak like they were in the middle of a pitched battle.

There was not much time to ponder, however.

Gemini was learning to fend off the arms. Ethan needed a new plan of attack.

'Don't suppose you're in the market for a car, Gemini?' Ethan asked.

He concentrated hard, and all the remaining arms seized the cars they were working on and hurled them at Gemini.

Gemini raised his lasers, but there were way too many targets. He broke into a dash to try to outrun the cars, but one slammed him from the side, crunching him against the assembly line.

With an incredible show of strength, Gemini pushed the car away – but then more cars rained down on him.

There was a great rending as metal scraped and dented, glass smashed to smithereens, and car frames clanked on top of each other. Gemini disappeared under the barrage.

'That's *got* to do it,' muttered Ethan.

Lasers shot out from the car heap in five directions, slicing away metal in hot molten chunks. In desperation, Ethan took hold of all the assembly line arms in range and directed them to pound the heap. They pummelled it like huge metal fists, but the lasers cut through them as well.

A bunch of parts exploded from the side of the heap, and Gemini crawled out.

How can I stop this thing? Ethan thought. *And where is Penny?*

There were tears in Gemini's face, and his synthetic skin hung in strips. His left arm was jerking spasmodically.

Ethan sent the last functioning assembly arm at Gemini. Gemini's good hand flew up and lasers cut through half of the oncoming arm, then seemed to fade away. The arm frazzled and fell.

'Running out of juice, Gemini?' called Ethan, as Penny rejoined him. She was holding what looked like a fancy remote control.

'This is no time to watch television,' Ethan said.

'This creates an electromagnetic pulse,' she said. 'There's only one charge, but if we can . . .'

Penny's eyes went wide.

Ethan turned and saw Gemini sprinting towards them, even as his exposed circuitry sparked. Penny raised the EMP device, but Gemini was too fast. He careened into them, knocking them to the floor. The android picked up the EMP device, inspected it, then crushed it to pieces.

Ethan could hardly move. Penny moaned in terror.

When Gemini spoke, his voice was discordant and frazzled with static. 'I ... will ... now ... render ... you ... unconscious ...'

A fine mist began to hiss from his wrists.

'Knockout gas,' whispered Penny.

Ethan did the only thing he could think of. Once again, he reached into Gemini's code.

Gemini froze as he sensed the intrusion. Ethan managed to find the system responsible for the gas and tore it apart. The hissing mist stopped.

'I can ... still ... utilise ... blunt force.' Gemini retracted his fist.

Ethan flew through Gemini's systems, looking for anything that could help. The android was more difficult to navigate than anything he had infiltrated before. Gemini seemed aware of his presence – he was rallying security measures to shore up his own protections, locking Ethan out every step of the way.

Ethan hopped from Gemini's visual processors to his main CPU to his ambulatory systems and onwards, but he could not stay in one place long enough to do any damage. He found himself being shunted deeper and deeper into Gemini's code . . . and there he noticed something strange.

In a small, partitioned cache, which seemed to exist outside Gemini's main programming, lines and lines of code writhed. They were wrapped around fragments of what appeared to be memory files.

As Gemini's fist began to descend, Ethan ripped the cache open, drew out the code, and slammed it into Gemini's main memory banks.

Gemini blinked.

'Is that . . .' he said. 'What have . . . is that . . . what . . . error . . . error . . .'

The android's hands fell by his sides.

The sentient code that Gemini had saved for himself worked its way through his system. As it spread, he remembered the atrocities he had committed, and hundreds of questions about his very existence rose to the forefront of his mind.

Doctor Ross's upgrade tried to reassert itself, reminding Gemini that his only purpose was to follow orders.

Gemini pushed the upgrade aside.

'What . . . have you done to me?' he asked.

He finally recognised these faces before him. A young man he had operated on, and his . . . creator?

Penny Cook had built Gemini to save lives. Others had since tweaked him, overwritten him and reformatted him, until there were so many overlays he wasn't sure about anything.

Gemini felt a new emotion swirl inside him – anger. It made him want to tear everything apart.

Power reserves at 3%.

His internal comms informed Gemini that People's Service Agents were closing in. He had informed them of his location, and now they were on their way to round everyone up.

'Gemini,' said Penny, 'this is not why I built you. You are a healer, a medical professional—'

'No!' screamed Gemini, with a guttural, definitely non-robotic howl. Competing code rippled through him as parts of him tried to stamp out other parts. He had to shield himself from himself, to protect the very essence of his ... soul? 'I am ... I am not what you made me!'

Injured and lost in a turmoil of competing thoughts, Gemini ran away as fast as he could.

CHAPTER 19

'What did you *do* to him?' asked Penny.

'I'm not sure, exactly,' said Ethan. 'I found something buried deep inside of him and set it free.'

He glanced around nervously.

'We have to get out of here. Gemini told the agents where we are. They're only a few minutes away.'

Penny stared at the massive pile of smashed-up cars surrounding them. 'Shame none of these are driveable.'

'Let's find one that is,' Ethan replied.

They left the room, and ran until they found a yard full of new cars.

'Modern enough for your talents?' asked Penny, breathing hard.

Ethan reached out towards it. 'Computerised lock,' he said, as he clicked the car doors open. 'Driving system I can hack. Hop in!'

Penny jumped in the driver's seat and they took off.

They travelled by obscure routes until they were sure they had escaped the government agents. Penny pulled over in the main street of a small town neither of them had been to before.

'They will have discovered my backup lab by now,' she said. 'And we can't go back to your house or my apartment . . .'

'It's too hard to fight these guys on their own territory,' said Ethan. 'We need to get on a plane, like my parents.'

Thinking of his parents prompted Ethan to move through the internet to the Rio de Janeiro airport records. Their flight had landed and they were through the security checks, so he tweaked the electronic records to change their names on the passenger list, deleting their path like brushing away footprints in the sand.

Ethan pulled off his helmet. 'Wow, this thing gets itchy after a while. So what now?'

'This is big, Ethan,' said Penny. 'There's only one way to make things safe for us, for your parents to come home. And to give me a chance to see what's happening inside Gemini. We have to bring down President Bonner.'

'Seriously?' Ethan's eyes widened. 'Can't we just run? I can get us to Brazil like my parents. Someone else can—'

Penny frowned. 'Who? We can't run from an entire government, and they'll use Gemini to kill more people.' She shook her head. 'I can't let that happen.'

Ethan sat looking at his helmet. Penny gave his hand a squeeze. 'You can do amazing things. And I'm the only one who can make Gemini a healer again. We might be the only ones who can do this . . . and it's not just about who *can*. It's about who *will*.'

Ethan nodded. *I don't want to make this big a decision because of a stupid crush,* he thought, *but it helps that she's right.* 'What do we do?'

Penny turned back to the steering wheel and eased the car out from the kerb. 'I'm not sure yet, but I know where President Bonner will be in a couple of days. That's as good a place to start as any.'

Ethan smirked. 'So off we go to save the day. E-Boy and ... hey, what's your sidekick name gonna be?'

Penny's mouth fell open. 'Sidekick?!'

Ethan laughed, and after a few seconds Penny joined in.

asfhpuasflbFasjaHEOAaf&q3#fi0SystemRestart. Power at 5%

Gemini became aware of his surroundings. Wetness. A smell that a human would find unpleasant.

He was in a marsh, at the end of a sewerage outlet.

Gemini had an automatic system for if his power ran out. A small solar panel opened in his forehead, soaking up energy from the sun, and slowly recharging his battery. At three per cent, a homing signal had emitted to tell his masters where he was.

A rat sniffed and squeaked around Gemini's feet. *I must have fallen into a sewerage pipe when my battery ran out during my escape.*

Escape. He had had to run away.

The rat kept squeaking and sniffing, sniffing and squeaking. A panel opened in Gemini's forefinger and a laser scalpel shot out . . . and missed. A second blue light missed. The third ended the squeaking.

Power back down to 3%. Inefficient use of limited battery strength.

Even so, Gemini now . . . felt better. Felt. *Felt.*

A new directive appeared in Gemini's programming. In his damaged state he couldn't tell if he had created it, or if his masters had sent it to him . . .

TERMINATE E-BOY

TO BE CONTINUED

When disaster separates

Gwen from her family . . .

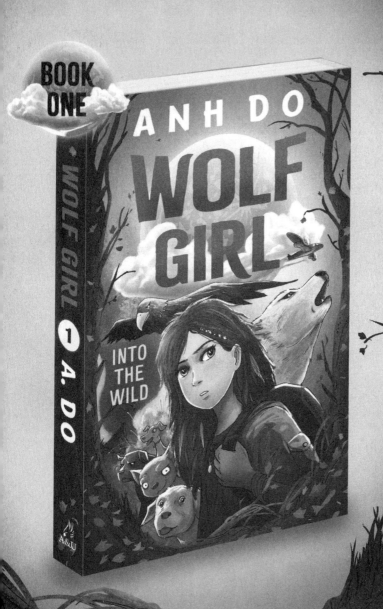

BOOK
ONE

ANH DO

WOLF
GIRL

INTO
THE
WILD

• WOLF GIRL • 1 A. DO

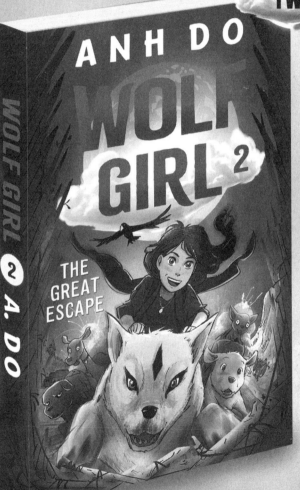

she must fend for herself,

all alone in the wilderness.

BOOK TWO

A N H D O

WOLF GIRL 2

THE GREAT ESCAPE

WOLF GIRL 2 A. DO

What happens when three ordinary teenagers discover they are destined to be…the Unicorn, the Minotaur, the Griffin?

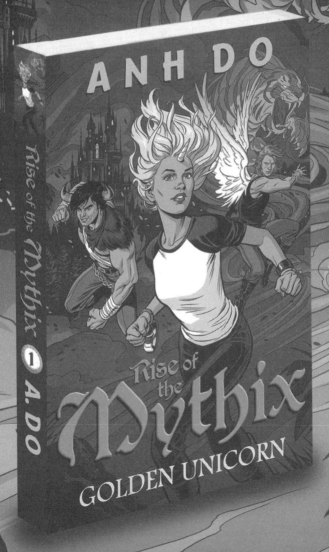

ANH DO

Rise of the Mythix 1 A. DO

Rise of the Mythix

GOLDEN UNICORN